The Saga of

Shakespeare Pintlewood

and the

Great Silver Fountain Pen

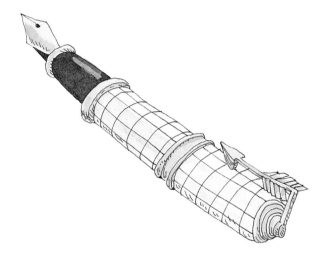

Written by

James H. Lehman

Illustrated by

Christopher Raschka

Brotherstone Publishers
Elgin, Illinois

Published by
BROTHERSTONE PUBLISHERS
1203 Lennoxshire Drive, Elgin, IL 60123

Printed in the United Stated of America

Library of Congress Catalog Card Number: 90-82303

Lehman, James H.
The saga of Shakespeare Pintlewood and the great
silver fountain pen/written by James H. Lehman;
illustrated by Christopher Raschka. p. cm.
Summary: A literary ant becomes a famous writer of
children's stories but gives it all up to travel through
the world telling stories directly to children.
ISBN 1-878925-00-8
[1. Ants - Fiction. 2. Animals - Fiction.
3. Authorship - Fiction. 4. Storytelling - Fiction.]
I. Raschka, Christopher, ill. II. Title.
PZ7.L   Sag 1990   [E]   90-82303

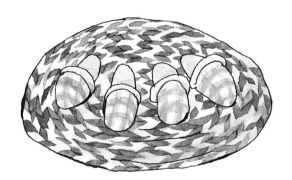

To Libby~
Best Wishes!
From
    Jim Lehman

Once upon a time there was an ant who liked to make up stories for children. His name was Shakespeare Pintlewood, but all the other ants called him Shakey for short.

Because he was very small, Shakey saw things the way little girls and boys do. To him people looked like giants and garage doors looked like castle gates, and so he was able to make up good stories.

But he did not know any children. There was no one to whom he could tell his stories. So he decided to write them down and put them in books.

The first thing he did was to order the best fountain pen he could find. It was a beautiful pen, silver with a gold clip and a sharp nib.

He had it delivered to his home. When it came, he laid out a clean sheet of paper and began to hoist the pen up in the air to write. It was very heavy and he grunted and strained, but he finally got it up.

He tottered to the top of the paper and started. The pen wavered and wobbled. Sometimes it fell over and flipped him up in the air.

Once too much ink squirted out, and he slipped and slithered around in it while the pen jiggled and danced and then fell over, upsetting the ink bottle and drenching him in a flood of ink that washed him over to the paper clips.

Wearily, he took out a clean sheet of paper and started over. It took him an hour and a half to write "Once upon a time," and when he was done, his back ached so badly that he took a bath and went to bed.

But the next morning he was at it again, staggering across the paper with the pen swaying like a drunken sailor.

At first he could write only ten or twelve words a day, but after a while he was up to fifteen and then twenty. After many weeks he finished his story.

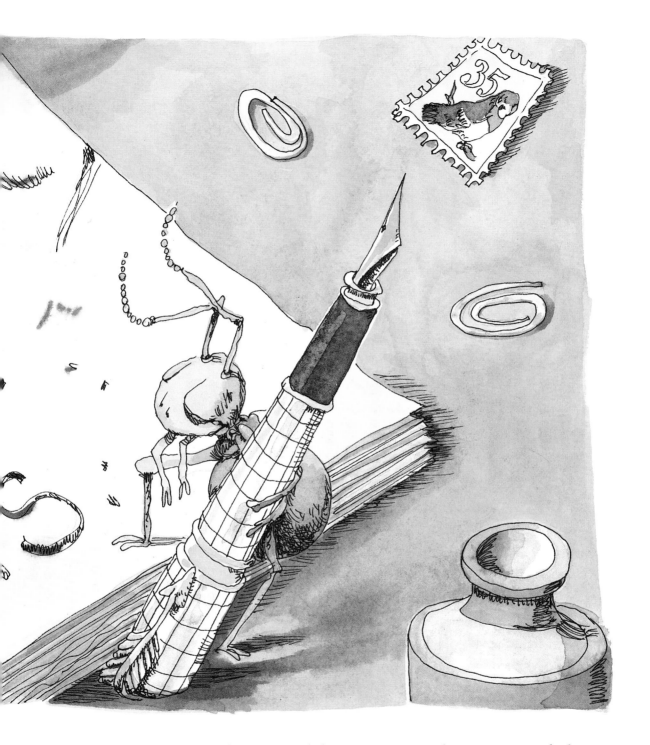

It was hard to read his writing because of the footprints and ink blots, but he was very proud of the story and sent it off to the people who make children's books.

They liked it and decided to make it into a
book. It was put into the bookstores, and it became a great favorite with all the boys and girls.
Shakey was pleased.

Shakespeare Pintle-wood wrote many more stories. They were hard work and each one took many hours, but they were good stories and they made him famous. He became a great literary ant. People threw banquets for him and gave him awards. He made lots of money. Everywhere he went people asked him to sign his autograph, and though it was hard for him, he always hoisted up his pen and did it.

SHAK
PINT

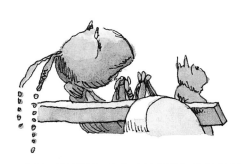

But Shakey wasn't happy. He still didn't know any children. Lots of children *read* his stories, and he was glad for that, but he never got a chance to *tell* his stories. So he locked up his home, lifted his fountain pen onto his shoulder, and started off on a long journey.

Whenever he came to a town, he searched for
the children. He gathered them around and told
them stories. Their eyes grew big and they fell
silent, listening closely. At the sad parts they
looked very serious and sober. At the exciting
parts they leaned forward or sat up suddenly.
They laughed. They cheered. They sighed.

When he finished, they asked for another and then another. The stories he told were even better than the ones he had written.

After the stories, he asked for a piece of paper, raised up his silver pen, and drew pictures of giants and castles and other scenes of mystery and delight. Then he put his pen on his shoulder and trudged on to the next town. The children loved his stories and pictures, and Shakey was very happy.

Shakespeare Pintlewood journeyed for many years. All over the world he could be seen, carrying his heavy pen. In cities children found him walking down sidewalks, dodging bicycles and

skateboards and stumbling over cigarette butts.
Out in the country they found him making his way
along dusty back roads, pausing to rest under the
honeysuckle or hitching a ride on a pick-up.

He became even more famous than before. Newspaper reporters wrote articles about him. His picture appeared on the cover of *Time* magazine. Preachers said he was a saint.

After years and years, Shakey grew too old
for the road. His pen was tarnished and worn.
His voice had grown thin and weary. His back
was too weak to carry the pen. Painfully and
slowly, he made his way home. There he sat,
never again telling a story or lifting his pen.

But now the children came to him. They sat with him for hours and they told *him* stories, and he would laugh and his eyes would shine.

Then they would ask if they could use the pen. He would shake his head eagerly. They would draw pictures while old Shakey looked on and nodded.

One day one of the children carved a tiny chair, fastened it to the top of the pen, and put Shakey in it. The ant rode like a king on his ancient silver pen while the children drew fierce giants and lovely old castles.

Those were the best years of
all for Shakespeare Pintlewood,
years filled with the laughter
and stories of children. When he
died, people all over the world
mourned him. But it was the
children who missed him most.

After Shakey was buried, his silver pen was given to a little boy, the child who had carved the chair. When the boy grew up, he became a writer and wrote many stories with Shakey's pen, but

the best story of all was the one he wrote about Shakey himself, and he called it "The Saga of Shakespeare Pintlewood and the Great Silver Fountain Pen."

An audio tape entitled
The Great Silver Pen and Other Stories,
featuring
"The Saga of Shakespeare Pintlewood and the Great Silver Fountain Pen"
and five more stories by James H. Lehman,
narrated by the author,
is available from your local bookstore or from
B R O T H E R S T O N E   P U B L I S H E R S
1203 Lennoxshire Drive, Elgin, IL 60123
Cassette ISBN 1-878925-01-6